For Marianne and Ciaran
M.W.

To Helen Walpole
B.F.

Printed in Italy
First U.S. edition
1 2 3 4 5 6 7 8 9 10

Library of Congress Cataloging in Publication Data
Waddell, Martin.
We love them / written by Martin Waddell; illustrated by Barbara Firth.
p.   cm. Summary: A dog and a rabbit become great friends.
ISBN 0-688-09331-0. — ISBN 0-688-09332-9 (lib. bdg.)
[1. Dogs—Fiction. 2. Rabbits—Fiction. 3. Friendship—Fiction.
4. Country life—Fiction.] I. Firth, Barbara, ill. II. Title.
PZ7.W1137We 1989
[E]—dc20   89-8226   CIP   AC

We Love Them

Written by
Martin Waddell

Illustrated by
Barbara Firth

Lothrop, Lee & Shepard Books
New York

In all the white fields
there was one rabbit.
It was lost.
It was small.
It lay in the snow.

Ben found it.

Ben barked.

We picked it up

and took it home.

Becky thought it would die,

but it didn't.

It lay with Ben.

Ben licked it.

Becky said that Ben thought

it was a little dog, and it thought

Ben was a big rabbit.

They didn't know they'd got it wrong.

Becky said we wouldn't tell them.

We called our rabbit Zoe.

She stayed with Ben.

She played with Ben.

We loved them.

Zoe wasn't little for very long.

She got big…

and bigger…

and bigger still,

but not as big as Ben.

But Ben was old…

and one day

Ben died.

We were sad and

Zoe was sad.

She wouldn't eat her green stuff.

She sat and sat.

There was no Ben for our rabbit,

until one day...

in the pale hay...

there was a puppy.

We took it home.

It lay down with Zoe.

Becky said our puppy thought

Zoe was a dog.

And Zoe thought

our puppy was a rabbit.

They didn't know they'd got it wrong.

Becky said we wouldn't tell them.

The puppy stayed.

The puppy played.

We loved him,

just like we loved Ben.

We called our puppy Little Ben.

But Little Ben got big…

and bigger…

and bigger still.

He got bigger than our rabbit

but not as big as old Ben.

Zoe still thinks
Little Ben is a rabbit,
and Becky says that
Zoe doesn't mind.
Becky says that Zoe
likes big rabbits.

Zoe and Little Ben play
with us in the green fields.
They are our dog
and our rabbit.
We love them.